This Walker book belongs to:

_____

_____

_____

First published 1987 by Walker Books Ltd
87 Vauxhall Walk, London SE11 5HJ

This edition published 2015

2 4 6 8 10 9 7 5 3 1

© 1987 Colin West

The right of Colin West to be identified as author/illustrator of this work
has been asserted by him in accordance with the Copyright, Designs and Patents Act 1988

This book has been typeset in Optima

Printed in China

British Library Cataloguing in Publication Data:
a catalogue record for this book is available from the British Library

ISBN 978-1-4063-6750-8

www.walker.co.uk

"Hello, great big bullfrog!"

Colin West

WALKER BOOKS
AND SUBSIDIARIES
LONDON · BOSTON · SYDNEY · AUCKLAND

"Hello, I'm a great big bullfrog," said the great big bullfrog.

"Hello, great big bullfrog!
Guess who I am!"

"I'm a great big rat,"
   said the great big rat
   to the great big bullfrog.

"Hello, great big rat!
Guess who I am!"

"I'm a great big warthog,"
said the great big warthog
to the great big rat
and the great big bullfrog.

"Hello, great big warthog!
  Guess who I am!"

"I'm a great big tiger,"
said the great big tiger
to the great big warthog
and the great big rat
and the great big bullfrog.

"Hello, great big tiger!
Guess who I am!"

"I'm a great big bear,"
said the great big bear
to the great big tiger
and the great big warthog
and the great big rat
and the great big bullfrog.

"Let's have
a great big
HULLABALOO!"

But the great big bullfrog
didn't want a great big hullabaloo.

He didn't feel
so great and
big any more.
He felt a tiddly
little bullfrog.

"Goodbye, everybody!"
said the not so great big bullfrog.

But suddenly...

"Hello, great
big bullfrog!
Guess who I am!"

"I'm a great big bumble bee,"
said the great big bumble bee.

"And I'm a great big bullfrog!"
 said the great big bullfrog.
"A great

    great

        great big bullfrog!"

Colin West knows that reading *"Hello, Great Big Bullfrog!"* aloud
can be great fun. He says, "The bullfrog could have a croaky voice,
the rat a squeaky one and the bear a deep one, for instance.
By the way, did you notice how the front endpapers are different
from those at the back of the book?"